Mai's Bus Ride

Story by Heather Hammonds
Illustrations by Sarah Davis

Mai and Rose were at the bus stop.
They were waiting for the school bus.

"I wish my mum could take me to school,"
said Mai.

Mai lived next door to Rose.
"Lots of children go to school on the bus,"
said Rose. "I will look after you."

Mai didn't want to go on the bus.
She felt scared.
When the bus stopped at the bus stop,
Rose and Mai and some other children got on.

A big boy got on, too.
Mai had never seen him before.

Rose saw her friends at the back of the bus.
"You can sit here in this empty seat,"
Rose said to Mai.
"I will go and sit with my friends.
You can't sit with us
because you are too young.
Only the big children
can sit at the back of the bus."

Then, the big boy sat down
in a seat across from Mai.

The bus went up a street
and past some shops.

Mai hoped they were on the right bus.
Her mum did not go this way
when she took Mai to school in the car.

If only Mai could ask Rose.
But Rose was talking with her friends.

Mai tried hard not to be scared,
so she looked in her school bag
for a book to read.
But her hands were shaking.

Just as she took the book out of her bag,
it slipped out of her hand
and slid under the big boy's seat.

"Oh, no!" cried Mai.

The boy picked up Mai's book
and gave it to her.
"Are you all right?" he asked.

"This is the first time
I have been on the school bus," said Mai.

“My name is Thomas,” said the boy.
“I go to school every day on this bus.
I like it because I can look out
the big windows,
and watch all the cars and trucks going past.”

When the bus got to school,
Thomas told Rose that Mai was scared.

"I am sorry, Mai," said Rose.
"Tomorrow, I will sit with you."

Mai smiled at Rose.
"I will be all right," she said.
"I think it will be fun
to go on the bus after all."